Ten Sho

Wordswort

a wordsw

by Diane Wordsworth

Baggins Bottom Books

Also by Diane Wordsworth

Marcie Craig mysteries
Night Crawler

Tarot Tales
The Ace of Wands
The Ace of Cups

Toni & Bart time-travel tales
Mardi Gras

Wordsworth Collections
Twee Tales
Twee Tales Too
Twee Tales Twee
Twee Tales More
Flash Fiction: Five Very Short Stories
Ten Short Stories: Wordsworth Shorts 1 - 10

Words Worth Reading
Issue 1: October 2021

Wordsworth Shorts
The Spirit of the Wind
The Most Scariest Night of the Year
The Girl on the Bench
Dancing on Ice
Happy Christmas, Santa
Careful What You Wish For
New Year's Revolution
One Born Every Minute
The Mystery of Woolley Dam
Martha's Favourite Doll
The Complete Angler
Alexandra's Ragtag Band
Pancake Race
The Phoenix Lights

Wordsworth Writers' Guides
Diary of a Scaredy Cat
Project Management for Writers: Gate 1 – What?

Watch for more at https://dianewordsworth.com.

Table of Contents

For Ian, always

Ten Short Stories: Wordsworth Shorts 1 – 10

Ten Short Stories: Wordsworth Shorts 1 – 10 is a Wordsworth Collection of ten short stories that have all previously been published as standalone Wordsworth Shorts.

1. *The Spirit of the Wind* has been published in *My Weekly, Twee Tales, Words Worth Reading* and *Twee Tales More.*
2. *The Most Scariest Night of the Year* has been published in *Words Worth Reading* and *Twee Tales More.*
3. *The Girl on the Bench* has been published in *Words Worth Reading* and *Twee Tales More.*
4. *Dancing on Ice* has been published in *Twee Tales Too* and *Twee Tales More.*
5. *Happy Christmas, Santa* has been published in *Twee Tales Twee* and *Twee Tales More.*
6. *Careful What You Wish For* has been published in *Twee Tales* and *Twee Tales More.*
7. *New Year's Revolution* has been published in *My Weekly, Twee Tales* and *Twee Tales More.*
8. *One Born Every Minute* has been published in *My Weekly, Twee Tales* and *Twee Tales More.*
9. *The Mystery of Woolley Dam* has been published in *Twee Tales Twee* and *Twee Tales More.*

10. *Martha's Favourite Doll* has been published in *Twee Tales Twee* and *Twee Tales More*.

1. The Spirit of the Wind

(This short story has been published in *My Weekly*, *Twee Tales*, *Words Worth Reading* and *Twee Tales More*)

Father O'Rourke was a chirpy fellow. He was well-fed, well-rounded and well into his sixties. He was also a popular character in this tiny hamlet in Kent, and the villagers were always calling on him to perform one service or another.

Tonight it was the turn of the McMahons, newcomers to the village but also the new landlord and his wife at the local pub.

The old priest sprinkled holy water at various intervals around the public bar in the Queen's Arms. Taking care not to splash any on the antique rosewood furniture, he muttered constantly to himself.

"I don't know," he chuntered. "Never had any complaints before..." a splash at the door, "... Old Ned's a friendly ghost... first time in thirty years I've ever been asked to exorcise him..."

"What was that?" interrupted Bernadette McMahon, a pretty young thing only recently married. "What did you say, Father?"

"Oh nothing, nothing," he replied. "Just a little prayer," then under his breath: "I pray Ned doesn't turn up tonight."

Bernadette and Patrick McMahon hadn't been in Major's Marsh long. Newly wed and newly qualified, they'd been sent to the sleepy hamlet on trial to run the Queen's Arms, an old coaching house owned by the brewery.

Patrick was great fun. He got on well with the locals and everyone liked him. Everyone liked his young wife too, she was just a little 'odd' at times.

Still, they both did a good job, it was nice to have a young couple around the place and she kept herself to herself – until Pat let slip the story of Old Ned that is.

"And he managed the pub for forty-five years..." he told her one evening. "He was so happy here during his life that when he died he chose to stick around..."

"Oh don't be daft," interrupted his wife. "There's no such thing as ghosts."

"But he's here –"

"How do you know? Has anyone ever seen him?"

"No but –"

"Has anyone ever heard him?"

"No but –"

"Well then. I rest my case."

"But they know he's here. He loves the place so much he keeps an eye on it, looks after it – and the people who live and work here.

"One year they discovered a fire had started in the kitchen," he continued. "It had been doused with water while everyone was asleep. Another time a burglar was shut in the cellar until morning even though no-one had locked the door.

"I tell you he's here."

"Well," she said finally when she could get a word in. "If you believe it so much we'll get the local priest in to remove him."

"You can't do that."

"Why not?"

"Because he's a friendly ghost."

"Rubbish," she retorted. "No such thing as a friendly ghost."

"You just said there was no such thing as ghosts," but she didn't hear him as she was already halfway up the stairs to bed.

Bernadette made the necessary arrangements the very next day and the Queen's Arms was granted a bar extension one night in October so the exorcism could take place.

Father O'Rourke didn't really want the job, but Mrs McMahon had her mind made up and would have gone outside the village if he'd refused. He thought that Ned would understand if it was someone he knew and stay away. So the old priest did his duty and turned up with all his bits and bobs.

They waited for three hours. Pat got fed up and went to bed but couldn't sleep. Ned didn't turn up much to Father O'Rourke's relief and Bernadette's satisfaction.

"See," she cried. "I told him there were no such things as ghosts."

Father O'Rourke collected together his things. "I'm sorry you've had a wasted journey, Father. Would you like a cup of coffee – or something stronger perhaps?"

"No thank you, Mrs McMahon," he replied glancing at the grandfather clock. "Three o'clock is well past my bedtime. I'll see you on Sunday though?"

"Oh yes, I'll be there," she walked with him to the door. "I'm sorry Pat won't be there too."

"That's all right," he said patting her hand. "Your husband has the faith, that's good enough for me."

"Goodnight Father, and thanks."

"Goodnight my child. God bless."

Bernadette closed the old, heavy door behind the old heavy man and slid the bolt home.

The noise echoed around the empty room as the fire collapsed for the night. She unplugged the fruit machines and Wurlitzer juke box, switched off the few lights that were still on and made her way to bed.

THE FOLLOWING EVENING a new fire danced brightly in the hearth. the wall lights were on low and the grandfather clock ticked steadily. Ale flowed freely and everyone talked about everything except the failed exorcism of the early hours. The locals were quite fond of Old Ned and didn't really want to think about what might have been.

"It's blowin' up for a bit of a storm out there," said Tom the grocer as he burst through the door. "I'll have my usual please, Pat," and he warmed his backside on the open fire.

"I'm sure it'll blow over," said Jack. He ran the Post Office. "They haven't forecast anything."

"That's just it," laughed Tom. "They don't know what to forecast so they don't bother."

"All the same, it's getting very dark out there."

"Well," said Pat. "It does get late early these days you know. Get some beer down you an' ye'll be fine." He chuckled softly at his own awful joke serving the drinks quite cheerfully. It had gone cold out – always good for business. Most people would far rather sit by a real fire supping real ale than stay at home running up their own electric bills.

By nine-thirty the bar had filled up nicely. Bernadette joined her husband pulling pints.

Soon the cosy front room at the Queen's Arms was heaving with bodies, all catching up on the news and gossip, which was much the same as on previous evenings, oblivious to the storm that was starting to rage outside.

Suddenly, the lights went out, the juke box – quiet though it was – wound down to a halt and the pumps failed.

"Who switched off the fruit machine?" someone wailed.

"S'all right," said Pat. "Stay where you are. I'll fetch some candles."

"But what're we going to drink?" asked someone else.

"We've plenty of canned and bottled stuff," assured Bernadette, amused by some people's sense of priority. "There might even be a keg or two in the basement." She soon got the drinks going again.

The pale firelight flickered, reflecting in thirty-or-so faces while Pat placed the candles strategically around the room. It looked so warm and friendly that Bernadette considered doing it more often. It didn't take long to entertain the villagers. Jack's wife, Beattie, sat herself down at the old upright and tinkled away at the worn piano keys until strains of 'Side by Side' and 'The Birdie Song' drifted out and along the lane above the sound of the wind.

Bernadette thought she could hear someone slowly clapping outside, but when she went to see, there was no-one there and the noise stopped. She served a few more drinks but when Pat heard it too she decided to investigate. "Probably the TV aerial or washing line flapping in the wind," she said as she walked around the bar counter.

"Here, I'll come with you," said Pat wiping his hands.

"You stay here and look after the customers. I shan't be long."

She left the joviality behind and peered around the front door into the darkness. Two huge oaks flanked the house. The wind had stripped bare any solitary leaves intent on surviving the autumn. The trees swayed precariously, their uppermost branches brushing the slates on the coaching house roof. They leaned dangerously into the building.

Shadows danced around the bottom of the trees until her eyes got used to the dark. Then she stepped out into the storm to see what, if anything, had worked itself loose. But she found nothing. A rather windswept and slightly wet Bernadette checked her watch and went back in to call time just as the power came back on.

"She timed that right, Pat," said Tom. "Goodnight to you both."

"'Night, Tom."

"Don't forget that fruit machine owes me money. Goodnight."

"See you tomorrow," said Jack finishing his pint and collecting his wife from the piano stool.

"Yeah, g'night," said Bernadette locking up behind them all. "We'll have taken a penny or two tonight," she said to her husband.

"Yes, and the electric bill won't be too high either."

They pulled the plugs, washed the glasses, turned off the lights and extinguished the candles. Both too tired to clear up completely after the previous night's escapade, they made their way to bed. In fact, they were both so tired they slept through the rest of the storm.

BERNADETTE AND PATRICK awoke the following morning to the sound of excited chatter outside and the huge brass knocker against the heavy front door.

"What is it?" called Bernadette jumping out of bed and throwing on her dressing gown. Pat did the same and together they stumbled down the stairs. On opening the front door they were greeted by half the village.

"What's up?" asked Pat squinting in the winter morning sunshine. The wind had dropped now.

"You're lucky to be alive," said Tom stepping down off the doorstep.

"Surprised it didn't wake you earlier," said Jack.

"Are you all right?" asked Beattie.

"Why?" asked Pat. "What's happened?"

"The two oaks," said Tom pointing. "They should have fallen onto the inn."

"But they went two completely different directions," continued Jack.

"They fell against the incline."

"It's a miracle," said Beattie. "They should have fallen onto the inn."

Pat and Bernadette stepped out into the sharp October air, pulling their dressing gowns around them. Indeed the two trees had fallen away from the house. Bernadette remembered watching them leaning over the house the previous evening. It was true, they should have fallen onto the inn.

"Jesus, Mary an' Joseph," exclaimed Bernadette crossing herself. "It really is a miracle."

"Actually," said Father O'Rourke pushing his way through from the back of the crowd. "Much as I'd like to believe it, I don't think it was a miracle."

"What makes you say that?" asked Pat.

"The trees were both chopped."

"You mean someone tried to kill us?"

"On the contrary. It probably saved your lives."

"But who would do such a thing?"

Everyone exchanged looks but no-one replied.

"I thought I heard a strange noise last night," said Bernadette.

"Yes, but there was no-one there," answered her husband.

"Then it must have been Old Ned," said Father O'Rourke. "Planted those trees himself. Must have broken his heart to do that, but at least the inn was saved." He was in a world of his own. "And to think I tried to exorcise him," he finished sadly, shaking his head.

At first this statement was met with stunned silence. But then, as if it were the most natural explanation in the world, the villagers bade the McMahons good morning and went about their business discussing something about Sevenoaks in Kent being flattened during the night.

"There's no such thing as ghosts," said Bernadette as she stomped back into the house.

Patrick exchanged a wink with the old man, followed his wife and closed the door.

the end

2. The Most Scariest Night of the Year

(This short story has been published in *Words Worth Reading* and *Twee Tales More*)

Georgia Lennard didn't have time to collect another fare. She had to get back to school to collect the kids. It was apparently the most scariest night of the year and she was taking them out. She flicked on the off-duty sign in her taxi and hightailed it in the general direction of the school.

The back streets were relatively empty at this time of day, being more likely to come alive with the less than salubrious night-life this quarter was famously known for. It wasn't a district you came to of an evening unless you were a gentleman or lady of the night. It wasn't really a district you'd choose to come to during the day either, to be frank. Georgia hated having to come here for customers, but it was a short-cut to everywhere else and if it saved time, then it saved money for Georgia.

She drummed her fingers on her steering wheel in time to the music on the car radio as the streetlights started to come on, and she thought ahead to the evening's shenanigans. It was Halloween. The kids loved Halloween. Once they'd had their tea, they were going out trick-or-treating. Georgia hoped that the weather would hold for them.

As she rounded a corner between a couple of industrial units that towered over the streets, Georgia slammed her foot on the brake. What was that in the middle of the road? She let the engine tick over as she wondered first if it was a pile of clothes and then if it was a sack of discarded kittens. It was the thought of kittens that made her choose to go and investigate further.

Georgia opened the door just as a fine drizzle started to fall. Pulling up the collar on her jacket, she carefully picked her way across the slippy cobbles. A shiver ran down her spine. She glanced around. *Creepy*, she thought.

Looking down at the pile of clothes she shivered again. It wasn't moving, so that meant it wasn't a sack of kittens... unless they'd all already died. She thought about examining the pile but shuddered at the thought. Did she really want to see a load of dead kittens? No, she didn't. But she squatted down anyway and used one of her long fingernails to move the material to one side.

A clown's face suddenly grinned at her, causing her to topple backwards with surprise and land on the wet ground. She was quick to get back up again and she stared at the face, feeling the backside of her jeans at the same time. When she saw that it was only a mask, she felt silly and looked around to see if anyone had seen her. There was no one there. Just Georgia, her taxi and the clown. What a strange thing to leave lying around.

She crept up to the pile of fabric once more and shone the torch on her mobile phone at it. Then she laughed. An embarrassed laugh.

"It's a puppet!" she said out loud. "A clown puppet." She looked at her surroundings again, to make sure that there really wasn't anyone else there, then she bent over and carefully picked the puppet up.

It was about the size of a child and it had strings attached to its head, hands and feet. She held onto the wooden slats and wiggled them around a bit, but she couldn't get the puppet to move for her. Running her fingers over it she realised it was all in one piece. *If the kids can work out how to use it, what a great thing for them to take out with them this evening,* thought Georgia.

She gave it a shake, lifting it completely clear of the ground, made sure there was nothing underneath it, and she stowed it on the back seat of her taxi. Then she climbed back into the front of the cab, hit the accelerator, and sped off towards the school. By now it was quite dark and her headlights sliced through the rain.

At a set of traffic lights, Georgia peered over her shoulder and jumped again. The clown was grinning right at her in the rear-view mirror. She shook herself. *Stop being daft!*

And then she felt one of her tyres blow out as the taxi skidded into the kerb.

"Dammit," she muttered, getting back out of the taxi. She didn't have time to wait for the AA. It would be quicker for her to change the wheel herself. It did make her even later, though. And the rain soaked right through her denim jacket.

WHEN THEY ALL EVENTUALLY piled into the house, Connor and Abbie dashed upstairs to change out of their school uniforms. Georgia left her denim jacket hanging on the balustrade and rubbed at her hair and face with a towel. Then she put their tea on (fish fingers, beans and chips) and arranged the puppet on the worktop where the kids would see it when they came back down to eat. She had a menacing feeling that she was being watched, but every time she turned around, only the puppet was there.

There was a death-curdling howl. Georgia looked down to see their black cat, Domino, arching its back and yowling at the puppet. Her yellow eyes were wide, her ears were flat and her tail had bushed up to more than twice its size.

"What's the matter, Dom?" said Georgia. "Don't you like it?"

She scooped the cat up into her arms, but Domino had her claws into her so fast that Georgia dropped her again. The cat scooted out of the kitchen, hissing and spitting and slipping all over the place on the floor tiles.

How odd, mused Georgia.

"What's wrong with Domino?" asked Connor, as usual the first one to report in for tea. He was still watching after her over his shoulder.

"She didn't like our new friend," said Georgia, waiting for Connor to see the puppet.

Connor's head turned to his mother, and then his eye caught the brightly coloured creature on the worktop. "Wow! What's that?" he said, dashing up to have a closer look.

"It's a puppet," said Georgia.

"It's ace," said Connor. "Can I have a go?" Without waiting for the go ahead, he picked the puppet up by the wooden things at the top of the strings. Within seconds he had the clown walking across the kitchen floor.

"Mum, the cat's just thrown up on the landing carpet!" called Abbie down the stairs.

"Clean it up, then!" her mother called back.

"Urgh!" said Abbie's voice.

But within a few moments Georgia could hear something rubbing on the carpet, and she smiled to herself. Her daughter was a good girl who'd do something if it needed doing rather than wait for someone else to do it.

Georgia was watching Connor making the puppet dance. She heard the upstairs toilet flush and then a tap running in the bathroom sink. Then her daughter's feet came thumping back down the stairs.

"Don't forget to let your sister have a go," said Georgia, turning to serve up their tea.

Connor wasn't listening. He was miles away, a massive smile on his face.

Abbie had Domino in her arms when she came into the kitchen, but the cat yowled again, jumped down, and scampered back up the stairs. "What's wrong with her?" asked Abbie. "Is there a full moon... Wow, what's that?" she said before anyone answered, running to her brother's side. Connor was demonstrating his new-found skills and he made the puppet wave at his sister. Abbie was delighted, and she clapped her hands. "Oh, can I have a go?"

Connor was reluctant at first, but he conceded and handed the mechanism to Abbie. Like her mother, though, she couldn't make head nor tail of it and she handed it back to her brother.

"Where did you learn to do that?" she said, taking her place at the table.

"Dunno," shrugged her brother. "Never tried it before."

"I'm sure you'll get the hang of it, Abbie," said Georgia, putting their plates on the table.

Connor carefully sat the puppet back down on the worktop, washed his hands, and sat opposite her. He picked up a squeezy bottle of tomato ketchup and smothered his baked beans.

Georgia turned up her nose. She'd never understood how anyone could put ketchup on beans when they were already covered in it.

She took her place at the table with the kids, pinching a chip off Abbie's plate.

"Hey!" said Abbie, but she didn't mind really.

"I thought you might want to take him out trick-or-treating," said Georgia, pointing the half-eaten chip at the puppet.

Connor's blue eyes grew wider. "Can we?" he said.

"That's a cool idea," said Abbie.

The house phone rang and all three of them exchanged surprised looks. No one ever called the house phone. It was there purely for the internet. And Great Aunt Mabel, of course, who refused to call any of them on their mobile phones. "Too expensive!" she always complained.

Georgia hoped that Great Aunt Mabel was all right. But when she picked up the receiver, there was no one there.

"Perhaps it's Dad struggling to get a signal," suggested Abbie.

That was possible. If ever their father did have trouble calling any of their mobiles, he did in fact call the land line, just in case.

She dialled 1-4-7-1, but the electronic voice at the other end told her that the last call was three weeks ago last Wednesday... And it was, indeed, Great Aunt Mabel.

"Hmm," she said, replacing the receiver on the wall-mounted cradle. As she started to clear up the kids' dinner plates, the phone rang again. This time there was just a hollow cackle before static took over again. She hung up, dialled 1-4-7-1 again, but got the same message as before. She stood there thoughtfully for a moment before seeing the clown's face looking right at her, making her jump. But when she checked again, his painted eyes were simply staring, unseeing.

Another shiver ran down Georgia's spine. She needed to pull herself together. This Halloween lark was getting to her.

THE KIDS WENT TO GET changed into their Halloween fancy dress outfits. Connor was a vampire, Abbie was a witch. Georgia had bought a black harness and lead for the cat, so that the witch's familiar could accompany them. However, of Domino there was no sign.

Georgia didn't bother dressing up, although she did change into some warm clothes. She was only there to supervise in any case. She wished that Terry wasn't working away that night. He always dressed up in a skeleton costume when he accompanied the kids. She hoped that the puppet would make up for him not being with them this year.

As it happened, the kids didn't seem to notice. Abbie carried the bucket for people to fill with sweets and chocolate and Connor walked the clown along, making him wave at passers-by as they passed by. Most of the neighbours seemed to like the puppet. It did make some of the older residents jump with fright, however. And even old Mr Jones at number forty-two who usually told them to clear off dropped some fifty-pee pieces into the bucket, eyeing the clown cautiously before slamming the door in their faces.

"Charming!" said Georgia.

"He always does that," said Abbie.

"Dad says he's a right old misery guts," said Connor.

THE KIDS WERE MORE than satisfied with their evening's haul as they shared everything out equally between themselves. They were only allowed to eat one chocolate bar each. Everything else went into goody tins on the kitchen counter. That was one of the things that Georgia liked about Halloween. She didn't have to buy any sweets for the next month.

As the kids made themselves comfortable in front of the telly, Georgia made her own dinner. She always ate her meals later than they did, because usually she ate with their dad. When he wasn't there, she stuck to it so that she didn't get too hungry the next time he was there.

She eyed the puppet, which Connor had sat back on the worktop, but this time it was sitting next to the goody tins. Georgia got up to fasten the lid back onto Abbie's goody tin, but when she sat down again at the table, it was unfastened again. "Hmm," she murmured, not taking her eyes off either the puppet or the tin.

The house phone rang again, but once again there was no one there, and once again 1-4-7-1 told her there hadn't been any callers for three weeks. When it rang again, she ignored it. But when the ringing stopped, she could hear Terry's voice.

I've had an accident, said the voice. *Help me! Help!*

She jumped up to pick up the phone, but all she could hear was that cackle again. She called her husband back, on his mobile, but it went to voice mail. And when she slammed the house phone back into its holder, she caught the puppet looking at her again, this time with an even bigger smile on its face.

Georgia shuddered. "You're creepy," she said, and the clown's head slowly started to move...

She grabbed at the puppet, dashed outside, and stuffed it into a wheelie bin, almost tripping over the cat.

"Oh, Domino!" she exclaimed. "You could have broken my neck!"

The cat hissed and spat at the wheelie bin and ran inside the open door into the house.

Georgia looked at the wheelie bin, then she wheeled it up the drive and left it at the side of the road. It was bin day the next day in any case and it would save her a job in the morning.

When she went back into the house, she saw Domino in her basket quite contentedly licking her paw. The cat paused for a moment to regard her human before carrying on.

A FEW HOURS LATER, after everyone had gone to bed, a car crawled along the road in the rain that had grown heavier throughout the evening. Terry Lennard had decided to come home tonight rather than tomorrow morning. He hadn't told his wife because he wanted it to be a surprise.

Domino was sitting on the windowsill looking out into the dark when she started to growl. She twitched her head and opened her eyes wide as she watched the lid of a wheelie bin slowly lift up. The clown clambered out and calmly went to stand in the middle of the road before melting into a pile of rags.

In his headlights, as he was turning into his driveway, Terry saw a pile of clothes lying in the road. Knowing how Georgia felt about people who abandoned kittens in sacks, he left his engine ticking over and went to investigate.

When he saw it was a puppet he decided to take it into the house. Georgia and the kids would be delighted when they saw what he had brought home when they got up in the morning.

the end

3. The Girl on the Bench

(This short story has been published in *Words Worth Reading* and *Twee Tales More*)

A male blackbird foraged for the last of the berries on the hawthorn while his mate tugged fat, juicy worms out of the ground. A squirrel scampered about, searching for acorns. His cheeks were already stuffed. If he could fit just one more in, then he'd go and bury his stash.

Golden leaves crunched underfoot, made yet more crunchy by a thin layer of morning frost still lingering from the previous night. Tamsin Price dragged her school bag along the floor before she sat down heavily on a bench beneath one of the trees. There was a nip in the air making her breath steam every time she opened her mouth. Making sure that her school coat was well beneath her bottom on the cold and icy bench, she pulled her collar up around her ears and watched the wildlife for a few minutes, smiling at their antics. They were very tame and not at all frightened of her.

She dug into her bag and arranged some of her belongings on the bench beside her. Mobile phone. Ear buds. Asthma inhaler. Mr Turford.

Teddy Turford was her oldest and her favourite teddy bear. She was a bit old for teddy bears, but this one went everywhere with her. She'd had him for ever, and he was small enough to fit into her school bag without anyone spotting him. She'd skived off school today, so it wasn't an issue, but Tamsin would die of embarrassment if the other kids found out about Mr Turford.

She breathed in the smell of wood smoke. There was a bonfire somewhere. She hoped that whoever it was had checked that there were no hedgehogs asleep under the pile before setting light to it.

After scrolling through her phone for a bit, she went to the story she'd bookmarked the day before that had popped up on Facebook. Not that she was old enough to have a Facebook account, but that was soon remedied simply by falsifying her birth date. Every year she moved her birth year back a year and by her next birthday, it would read the right date at last.

It was the headline that had caught her eye:

BOY'S ATTEMPTED SUICIDE BLAMED ON SCHOOL BULLIES

SHE ALWAYS FOUND IT a bit spooky that Facebook seemed to know *everything* about you. Apart from her real birth date, of course. But generally, if she Googled anything or if she followed a link to somewhere, within seconds Facebook would target her with adverts and stories based on what she'd just been looking at.

Tamsin shuddered. According to her dad it was Big Brother watching everything that everyone did. She had no idea who Big Brother was, but he seemed Very Important, and almost all-seeing. She hoped he couldn't really see everything.

She'd read the story a few times the day before and now she read it out loud to Mr Turford. The words had hit a nerve. The story said the boy had been wagging school. Just like Tamsin was right now. The name-calling had really got to him, and when things started to get physical, he started to skive off school. Unable to face going back to school, he'd tried to cut his wrists. But he hadn't cut deep enough and now he'd have scars on the insides of his arms for the rest of his life. The story didn't mention the boy by name, but it did say that he was at a school in Birmingham. Tamsin's school was in Doncaster, so there was no chance that she might know him.

Tamsin sighed and picked at a scab on her knee. It wasn't quite ready yet and she winced at the sharp pain. She wiped away a small drop of blood with a tissue. "How painful would it be to slice at my own arm with Dad's Stanley blade?" she asked her teddy, tucking the soiled tissue back into her coat pocket. She didn't really want to think about it. "There must have been a lot of blood."

She shuddered again. There were too many similarities between the story on Facebook and the real story in her own life. She frowned as she tried to remember when the bullying at her school had first started.

"Probably the first week of the new school year," she said. Though try as she might, she couldn't pinpoint what it had been over. Was it the hockey boots? She furrowed her brow as she tried to remember. Yes, it was something about hockey boots.

Carey Parkes had told JoJo Skinner that JoJo could have Carey's old hockey boots. Everyone knew it was because JoJo was one of the best hockey players in their year but without a proper pair of boots, she wouldn't be allowed to play in the inter-school tournament. The rumour was that JoJo's parents couldn't afford to buy her a pair of her own. Even if the other girls didn't like her very much, they still wanted JoJo in the team because, more than anything, they wanted to win the trophy.

And then, for some reason, JoJo had helped herself to the boots from Carey's locker, which wasn't even locked, and when they saw her in them in the playground, Carey and all of her friends had laid into JoJo. it had started with just calling her names. But before long they were poking fun at her family's lack of money, following her home, spitting at her, pulling her hair, accusing her parents of being junkies. It had gone on for weeks, but not once did JoJo report Carey and her friends to the teachers.

And then yesterday, JoJo didn't turn up for school and Tamsin had seen the story on Facebook.

Why had JoJo helped herself to the boots? Why didn't she wait for Carey to just give them to her? Did anyone even ask her? Maybe it had just been a misunderstanding. Or did Carey tell her to take them?

More to the point, though, why had Tamsin jumped on the bandwagon and joined in? It wasn't really any of her business.

Tamsin shook her head. She wasn't a bully. "I'm not a bully!" she told Mr Turford. But she'd given in to the peer pressure at school and she'd sided with the bullies instead of sticking up for JoJo. She'd joined the others when they ganged up on her. Tamsin was very much a bully.

What if JoJo tried to kill herself? What if she tried to cut her own wrists? Apart from not wanting that on her conscience, Tamsin didn't think it was worth it, especially over a pair of hockey boots.

Tamsin stuffed all of her belongings back into her bag and tucked Mr Turford in too, then she swung the bag over her shoulder and made her way back down the hill towards school.

But she didn't turn in to the school entrance. Instead, she carried on walking until she reached JoJo's house. She knew which one it was because she'd followed her all the way there with the others.

Tamsin hesitated at the gate. She looked at the clean and tidy frontage. Taking a deep breath, she pushed the gate open and marched right up to the front door, rapping on the shiny red painted woodwork until her knuckles hurt.

A lady answered, who Tamsin assumed was JoJo's mother.

"Is JoJo there?" said the girl.

"She's not very well at the moment," said the woman. "She's in bed with the flu. Can I give her a message?"

"Yes, please tell her that Tamsin dropped by, and... and..."

"And?" said the pretty woman.

Tamsin pulled the bear out of her bag and held it out to JoJo's mum. "Tell her that she can borrow Mr Turford until she's better... and that I'm sorry."

the end

4. Dancing on Ice

(This short story has been published in *Twee Tales Too* and *Twee Tales More*)

Dan's heart sank to the pit of his stomach. These were yet more of the times he missed his late wife, not having her there for the girls. He'd promised his oldest daughter a treat of her choice for getting another sticker at school, and Suze had chosen ice skating.

"Loads of my friends are going," she'd said. "And it looks so easy on television."

Easy?! Pah! Pull the other one. Dan remembered his own attempts at ice skating only too well. While most of his friends were trialling for the ice hockey or speed skating teams, poor Dan was spending most of his time cold, wet, bruised and on his backside. Not to mention the ego-bashing and leg-pulling he'd also experienced.

Ice skating never was and never would be for him. But he *had* promised...

"Can I go too?" asked his younger daughter Matty.

Dan wasn't sure if there was a minimum age or not for ice skating at the local rink. He had a dim and distant recollection that there was a minimum age for sub-aqua diving, but he didn't remember anything about ice skating.

"Tallulah's little sister goes with her and she's six, the same age as Matty," said Suze, coming to the rescue – or was she banging yet another nail into his coffin? There went using Matty as an excuse not to go.

"Don't you need your own skates?" he asked, helplessly clutching at straws. Even he remembered the old floppy hire skates that provided no support for the ankles. They were creased and worn, they smelled to high heaven, and he was sure you could catch verrucas from them too.

"Oh, Daddy," admonished Suze. "Everyone knows you can hire skates, but Tallulah has a spare pair if I want to borrow them."

"We can't all borrow them, though, can we?" he said, resigned.

And he made the necessary arrangements for the three of them to go on one of the public sessions as well as making an appointment to see an instructor afterwards.

The box office and foyer had changed a lot since he'd last been there. It was more like the swish entrances to some of the larger leisure complexes or even shopping centres. In his day it had just been a scruffy hatch in the wall, a dodgy looking plain-clothes door, and a single window display advertising a handful of skate-wear. Now there were food court booths, several boutiques, and a small amusement arcade. It didn't feel as seedy as it had the last time he'd been. They'd also sold half of the building to one of the big chain supermarkets, and they'd extended upwards to create a private fitness club. And it was much more illuminated and heated.

The biggest surprise were the hire skates. Gone were the old red (for girls and ladies) and black (for boys and men), worn leather floppy, scruffy skates. Instead they were of a much more rigid material, plastic almost, and in some of the brightest, fluorescent colours he'd ever seen. They could also choose between figure skates with the brake at the front, or hockey skates without.

Already, when he tied the laces that surprisingly didn't break, nor were they knotted where previously they had broken, his ankles felt much more supported. Gingerly, he got to his feet and, other than a bit of a wobble, he was able to walk to the gap in the perimeter without falling over.

"Hey!" he announced, quite proud of himself. "I can stand up." Then he landed, with a bump, on the hard floor, on his bum, causing the girls to chortle with laughter.

Both Suze and Matty took walking in the skates in their stride. They watched from the seats for a few minutes before taking the leap. Dan tentatively stepped onto the ice first, immediately clinging to the side wall, and one-by-one helped his daughters do the same. A few desperate moves and they were standing up, if in a bendy kind of way, then the three of them took a few quick glidey moves.

Dan, as expected, was the first to land on the ice, but the girls thought it was hilariously funny and they all burst into more fits of laughter.

"Hey, Suze!" shouted a voice, and Suze's friend glided towards them looking very graceful. She had everything, all the gear, white figure skates, American tan thick denier tights, a fuchsia pink skating dress with a little jacket, and matching fluffy earmuffs and gloves. Her own little sister, dressed almost identically, but in acid orange, followed her.

"Hold our hands," Tallulah said.

"We'll take you around," said little Natasha.

"Can we, Dad?" asked Suze.

"Can we?" echoed her sister.

It sounded perfectly fine to him, and they'd never be far out of sight. Plus, it would give him chance to find his own ice legs without the embarrassment of his little girls watching him.

"Yay!" they cried, and off they went. Matty fell over almost immediately and Dan wanted to dash to her side. But she was soon up on her blades again, laughing, and off they went – again.

He clung to the side as he watched them complete a couple of circuits before bravely launching himself a few feet away, and he promptly lost his balance.

Dan's ankles were aching a bit with the unfamiliar strain. He'd not long recovered from a nasty fall on the snow in which he'd twisted one of his ankles. He flexed both feet a bit, bent down to tighten the laces, and tried again...

... and, actually, he managed a lot better than he thought he would. By the time he was able to carefully follow the four children, he was enjoying conquering the skates and wishing he'd pursued it when he was younger and more fearless than his sensible, adult self.

When it was time to take their skates back and meet the ice-skating instructor, the girls came back squealing with joy. Both Suze and Matty had taken to the ice like ducks to water – or penguins to ice – and their friends had even taught them a few easy dance steps.

Tallulah and Natasha swirled off in a flash of colour to join the others, spinning around the ice. Dan noticed that quite a lot of the children were wearing skating outfits, even some of the boys looking smart in their black trousers, white shirts and bow ties. Everyone else was either in tracksuits or regular jeans.

What looked like one of the coaches was headed in their direction.

"Do you want lessons or not?" he asked the girls, to another chorus of sing-song yeses. The attractive skating instructor smiled a beaming smile at them.

"Well?" she asked. "What did you think?"

"They really enjoyed themselves, thanks, and would love to have proper lessons."

"Really? That's great," she said, turning the smile on the girls.

"Er, do you teach adults too?" he spluttered out, surprising himself.

"Yes, we do," she said. And as she turned that stunning smile towards him he felt himself go slightly weak at the knees again, but this time it was nothing to do with the ice...

the end

5. Happy Christmas, Santa

(This short story has been published in *Twee Tales Twee* and *Twee Tales More*)

It was Christmas Eve and Faye had just been to *Toby's,* an expensive jeweller in town, to pay the last instalment on Billy's Christmas present. It had cost a fortune and he wasn't really into jewellery, but he'd already told her he'd like a nice slide for his tie for when they went out. Faye knew he'd adore the eighteen-carat gold ornament with the diamond-encrusted initials F&B entwined on it. It was something they'd discussed. She couldn't resist it and ordered one straight away on instinct. They didn't keep them in stock as they were classed as personalised.

But now it was ready to take away. The young shop assistant wrapped the gift beautifully, first in a little cardboard box and then with *Toby's* own personalised gift wrap.

Faye clutched the box in her sweaty palm and thrust it deep into the pocket of her old faithful winter coat. Luckily, as she waved goodbye and left the shop, there was a bus just pulling away from her stop. She jumped on it, just in time, and chose a seat about halfway along. It was only a single decker but there weren't many people on it. Most shoppers were probably still in town looking for last-minute presents.

As she sat there on the bus, trundling over the bumpy, uneven road surface, Faye's mind drifted back to the jewellers. She remembered the chests and windows full of trays of lovely rings, engagement rings. It would be really nice if that was what Billy had in mind this Christmas. After all, they had been together for three years now!

She glanced around the bus at her fellow passengers to see if she recognised anyone.

She didn't know the young mother battling with two very excited, very hyperactive, children. It seemed they'd just been to see Father Christmas. No such thing, of course, but it was such a shame that the children should have to find out one day.

Nor did Faye know the little old lady with the two white poodles. Poor things, they'd just been clipped, and in the winter too! Faye shivered at the thought and snuggled down into her lovely coat.

Two rows in front of her sat a familiar bulk. He was wearing a thick, dark grey woollen overcoat and a very strange red and white furry hat. Oh yes, there were always loads of these around at this time of year, but this one was different somehow, more luxurious, expensive even – and it sparkled too. Must have been the wet air outside making it shine, the atmosphere clinging in droplets to the Santa-hat.

Whoever it was, he was probably drunk, or a Christmas strippagram perhaps, keeping the silly hat on while he travelled on the bus. Maybe he was just cold, for he nestled deep inside the coat and looked half asleep.

When she got up for her stop Faye tried to get a better look, but his collar was turned up against the elements and his already well-hidden face was turned to the window as he stared long and hard at the view outside. Just as she was jumping down from the bus, however, she caught sight of more Santa-hats on the back seat, but it was too late for her to see if she recognised anyone there.

It wasn't until Faye got off the bus, though, and walked a few yards down the road that she noticed the package had gone. On inspection of her well-worn coat pocket she discovered, with dismay, a huge hole.

Not to worry, she thought. It would be in the lining somewhere. She examined the lining but there was a hole in that too. The next step was easy. Faye panicked!

She rifled through her handbag and shopping bag in the vain hope that she might have placed it elsewhere subconsciously whilst dreaming.

But no packet. She scoured the pavement and rummaged through the gutter. Fortunately, there had been no snow yet, although it had been forecast. Nevertheless, it still didn't turn up.

The package definitely wasn't in the vicinity, so Faye crossed the road and waited patiently for the return journey of the bus on its way back to town. If it wasn't on the bus, then it must be at the shop.

Presently the bus returned, and Faye climbed on.

"Has anyone handed in a small package?" she asked the driver who simply shrugged his shoulders. "Well do you mind if I check under the seats then?"

"You'll have to pay your fare."

"But I paid my fare earlier. I only want to see if I dropped a small package, then I'll get off..."

"It's the insurance, see," grunted the driver. "Ain't insured if you don't pay your fare."

"But..."

"Rules is rules, sorry."

Yeah, thought Faye snatching at her purse. You really look sorry. "And a Merry Christmas to you too, pal!" she said. But the driver just shrugged and pulled away.

Faye felt a complete idiot crawling around the dirty floor and up the aisle, searching beneath the seats. She was certainly getting some weird looks from the festive passengers on the now full bus. But still no package.

Faye was certain she had the box with her when she left the shop earlier, but just to make sure, when they got to town she went in. "Did I drop my package in here earlier?" she asked the young lad.

"Not that I know of." Seeing Faye's disappointment, he continued. "Or at least no one handed it in."

"Oh," said Faye.

"You're welcome to have a quick look around if you want."

Faye smiled bravely and proceeded to search the floor, behind the door, under the mat...

"You bought the diamond initial tie slide, didn't you?" Faye nodded. "Been very popular that particular range. Your diamonds were insured..."

"Does that mean I can get another one?" she asked brightening briefly, but the lad shook his head.

"Sorry, but even if you could, you'd have to order it. We don't keep the personalised stuff in stock I'm afraid, except for the display ones. No, you'll have to fill in a form." He handed Faye the piece of paper. "And you'll get a full refund once they've processed it."

Well, that was something at least.

"Would you like to buy anything else instead, for now?"

"Sorry, no money."

"Oh well, have a Happy Christmas anyway," said the lad. Faye knew that she wouldn't. She didn't even have enough money to buy Billy a box of chocolates.

Faye thanked the young assistant for his help rather dejectedly and plodded homeward in the fast-receding daylight.

As she reached their house the promised snow began to fall and a soft, warm glow welcomed her through the front window from the dancing living room fire.

Billy had put the tree up, decorated it and built the fire, and then fallen asleep in the armchair. Faye took in the scene. As she removed her coat, Billy stirred, and some soot tumbled down the chimney.

"You're home then?" he asked.

"Mmm."

"Where you been? I was starting to get worried."

"You really looked worried," she snapped but then reminded herself that wasn't fair as it wasn't Billy's fault she'd lost his present. She was about to apologise when she noticed the tiny gift-wrapped box in *Toby's* own wrapping paper suspended from a branch on the tree. Then she noticed the dark overcoat and Santa-hat strewn across the settee.

"You were on the bus!" she accused.

Billy gave her a sheepish grin. "I didn't think you'd noticed, you were in such a dream, thought I'd got away with it."

"But..."

"I couldn't believe it when I saw you go into *Toby's*. I didn't want to spoil your surprise so dived into the nearest open doorway so I could make my getaway before you emerged. Unfortunately, the old bloke thought I looked a bit suspicious so I had to buy one of those silly hats.

"I escaped just as the bus pulled up outside. Thought I'd missed you too till you climbed on at the last minute. But, like I say, you were in a dream. Thought you'd seen me as you got off, though. I was sitting at the back."

"But the present..." she pointed to the parcel on the tree and noticed there was an identical one hanging next to it.

"Yes, fancy us going to the same place."

"But I lost it."

"Yes, yes, 'course you did. Where you been anyway."

"Looking for the present."

"But it was here, on the table."

"It couldn't have been."

"Well it was."

Faye must have dropped the package and Billy picked it up, but he didn't want her knowing it.

"Why didn't you get off at our stop then?" asked Faye.

"Cos I didn't want you to see me."

Faye remembered the matching packages from the jewellers and grinned.

"Can we open our presents now?" she asked, excited about trying on her new ring.

"If you like," he replied, retrieving them both from the tree. "It is Christmas Eve. Hope you like it."

"You too."

As Billy opened his parcel a wide grin spread across his face.

"D'you like it?"

"Just what I wanted. Come on, it's your turn."

Faye tore frantically at her own present, eager to see if the ring would fit.

It wasn't a ring but something much nicer. There, on a soft nest of white cotton wool, lay a beautiful eighteen carat gold chain with the diamond-encrusted initials F&B entwined on it. They could wear the matching pair later on in the evening at the Christmas party they were going to.

"I was going to buy you a ring," said Billy. "But I didn't think you'd like that as much, and you always said what a nice idea the initials were." Okay, so he still didn't know her as well as he liked to think, but the necklace was lovely.

"This is perfect," she said running into his arms. "Happy Christmas, Billy." As Faye hugged him tightly she glanced over his shoulder through the window.

Standing beneath a streetlight, in the softly falling snow, was an old, grey-bewhiskered, slightly plump man. He was wearing a dark grey woollen overcoat and a very strange red and white furry hat. There were always loads of these around at this time of year, but this one was different somehow, more luxurious, expensive even – and it sparkled too. His hands were stuffed into the pockets of a red suit he wore beneath the overcoat.

His withered features crinkled into a big, beaming smile and he winked before turning and walking into the night.

"And a Happy Christmas to you too, Santa," whispered Faye.

the end

6. Careful What You Wish For

(This short story has been published in *Twee Tales* and *Twee Tales More*)

Petra was on a roll.

"Do we have to come boring Christmas shopping with you? Do I?" she whined.

Molly sighed. Her little girl was already growing up too quickly, already losing the joy of childhood. Oh, she knew it would happen eventually, knew it would come one day. And she really didn't want to stifle the teenager. But if she could just hold onto the child for just one more Christmas...

"No, you don't have to come with me at all, but I'd like it if you did. It would be nice to do something together as a family and I won't be able to control your brother all on my own with parcels and packages to battle with." Not to mention the weather, she thought to herself. "You'd be helping me out too."

"But if I don't come with you, you'll be able to get my present as well." The fifteen-year-old gave her mother one of those sarcastic little smiles, the kind that barred straight, white teeth in a flash before her pretty little face returned to that supercilious teenage mask.

"I've already got your present – "

"Have you? What is it? Where is it? Was it on my list?"

Too late Molly realised she'd walked into one of her daughter's traps, and she laughed. Perhaps her little girl wasn't growing up so quickly after all. It didn't take much for Petra to resort to childishness again if she thought she was getting something.

The children knew that Molly couldn't afford to get them very much since their father had left home and she'd gone back to work. The upside, however, was that they had two Christmases, two birthdays each, and two summer holidays. And really, Petra was very good, helping out around the house a lot more than other girls her age – according to Petra.

Molly tried again. "Surely you haven't already got all of your own presents?"

"I have to get Dad something. And Gran. But I've got all the others."

Molly smiled. "Really? Have you got mine? What have I got?"

Petra laughed. "Honestly, Mum. And you wonder where I get it from?"

The girl chewed on her bottom lip and curled a lock of hair around her right forefinger. Molly braced herself for the bribe she knew was about to come.

"Can Sofia come as well?"

Was that all? Sofia was Petra's best friend from school.

"I don't have a problem with that. But Toby will probably want to bring a friend too."

Molly sighed again, this time at the prospect of two boisterous ten-year-olds to control. But then she thought it might actually be quite a nice day out for all of them. The true spirit of Christmas.

AS IT HAPPENED TOBY didn't want to bring a friend after all.

"Just cos Petra's a big sissy girl who needs someone to hold her hand doesn't mean that I do too."

The usual sibling bickering was often highly amusing, but Molly hoped it wouldn't stress her any more on what was already going to be a tiring day. Petra, however, as it happened, was far too busy being all grown-up in front of her friend to retaliate – beyond poking out her tongue.

They arrived bright and early and Molly managed to park up without difficulty. She was surprised, though. This was a Saturday morning after all, only two weeks before Christmas, and there was hardly anyone about.

Sofia said: "They probably do all their shopping online now. That's what we did."

Not a bad idea, thought Molly. But she actually enjoyed Christmas shopping. It was all part of the fun. Tramping around cobbled streets wrapped up against the cold, listening to a choir singing or a brass band playing, people you don't know smiling at you, wishing you a Merry Christmas, the smell of mulled wine, and chestnuts roasting in an open oven. That's what it was all about, and The Shambles was the best place to do it in too. You could always find something special. They each found Molly's mother something nice, apart from Sofia of course.

"Who fancies a hot mince pie with cream?" Molly shouted.

"Me!" sang both of her children. However, when Sofia pointed out that she was watching her waistline and sweet stuff gave her zits, Petra started to falter.

"Look," said Molly. "It's only one mince pie and I promise you we'll work it off later – though with the walking we've done so far, we must already have something in the bank." She'd spotted a poster on a wall earlier and decided it would be the best way to end what had turned out to be a fantastic day.

They took their packages to the car and hid them safely in the boot, went and had their hot mince pies, then Molly led the way back through the crowds that had gradually increased, back through The Shambles to the castle.

"Wow!" exclaimed Toby when they got there.

"Cool!" said Petra.

Sofia grinned at Molly. "An outdoor ice rink," she said.

Yes, the health and safety party poopers hadn't closed this one down.

They hired some boots and followed everyone else around the rink in circles to the sound of the latest, and many of the much older, Christmas hits. They giggled when one of them lost their balance and helped each other up off the ice when they fell over. Molly knew that she would ache all over in the morning, but she didn't care. It was worth it just to see the children being children again at Christmas.

"Don't leave the ice rink without telling me first," she called, as the three of them wobbled off to explore and make new friends.

Left to her own thoughts and devices for a while, she found herself wishing she had a grown-up to share some of the fun with too, someone to share this special day, someone to hold her hand, someone to catch her when she slipped. A little voice inside her head whispered: "Be careful what you wish for," and she shook herself. Been there, done that. Didn't work. And besides, she had the children to consider.

Molly skated off to find herself a hot chocolate. There were booths and kiosks placed all around the rink perimeter so she didn't even need to leave the ice.

The girls and Toby all seemed to reconvene at once, Petra and Sofia babbling on about two boys they'd met, and Toby dragging a new friend behind him.

"Mum," he cried, trying to also concentrate on staying upright. By the amount of ice on his clothes and the number of wet patches, he'd already come a cropper more than once. "This is Luke. His dad's a photographer for the local paper." Molly caught sight of an apologetic looking man trailing at the heels of Toby and his new friend. "He's the same age as me."

"His dad or Luke?" laughed Molly.

"Luke's dad wants to take a picture of us all. Can he, Mum? Can he?"

Molly met the eyes of Luke's dad over her own son's shoulder.

"May I?" he smiled. "You're all wearing such wonderful colours, I thought when I first saw you it would make a smashing photo."

"Why not?" agreed Molly.

"Cool," said Petra. "Will we get a copy?"

"Sure," said Luke's dad. "If your mum lets me have her phone number."

"If she doesn't I will," said Petra. "It's about time she had a man in her life again."

"Petra!" admonished Molly, feeling herself flush.

"Really?" teased Luke's dad, meeting Molly's eye again.

Be careful what you wish for, Molly reminded herself. Seeing her discomfort and embarrassment, though, Luke's dad set about arranging the photograph, making a huge fuss of them all.

Molly hissed out of the corner of her mouth to Petra: "That was very naughty. He might not even be single."

Petra smiled and poked her tongue out again, then made a great show of giving Luke's dad their phone number *and* Molly's mobile number.

"I'll let you know when it appears in the paper," said Luke's dad to Molly, who was making leaving noises now.

"Thanks."

"Oh, and by the way..."

"Yes?"

"I am."

"You are what?"

"Single," he winked.

the end

7. New Year's Revolution

(This short story has been published in *My Weekly*, *Twee Tales* and *Twee Tales More*)

S *tig* arrived at the Southam's home, just in time for Christmas.

"What's that?" Molly asked of her eleven-year-old son.

"He's a stick insect," replied Toby.

"Yes, I can see that. But what is it doing here?"

"Miss asked for volunteers to look after the animals over the Christmas holiday."

"And you volunteered us, right?"

"Right."

"I see." Molly regained her composure. She couldn't very well send it back, could she? And it could have been worse: he could have brought home a nice cuddly rat, or a snake in a tank. "And what does it eat?" she asked, peering at the bright green creature through the ex-pickled egg jar. Someone had thoughtfully provided an ex-stocking leg for the lid too.

Toby put on his big, grown-up voice and recited what he had clearly learned in class. "The stick insect eats the foliage of plants, shrubs and trees, usually at night. Privet will do."

"I see," said Molly again, picturing her prized privet being gnawed to shreds by this... insect... "Does it have a name?"

"Stig."

"Stig?"

"Yes. We couldn't make up our minds between 'Stick' or 'Twig', so we called him 'Stig' instead."

"And does 'Stig' have any friends?"

Toby frowned, shook his head, and took a deep breath. In that matter-of-fact voice of his, he recited from his lessons once more. "In some species the male is rare. So the female reproduces an exact replica of herself without mating."

Molly shook her head and laughed, while at the same time marveling at her son's knowledge. "We'll leave him on the windowsill then above the draining board, all right?" Toby nodded. "Just so long as you look after him."

"Oh I will," he agreed, though Molly wasn't so sure. After all, who looked after the stray kitten he had found one day? Who fed and cleaned out his rabbits? Who returned his slugs and snails and all sorts of other creatures to the safety of the garden when he tired of examining them in the kitchen? Molly did. "And keep it away from Petra. You know how she hates creepy crawlies."

ON THE DAY BEFORE CHRISTMAS Molly frantically rushed around the place trying to get ready for work. It was the busiest day of the year at the department store in town where she worked. Her ex-husband was coming to take the kids shopping. Toby was getting dressed in his room and Petra was hogging the bathroom, again.

"Petra! Will you get a move on in that bathroom," she screamed up the stairs to her sixteen-year-old daughter. "Some of us have to get to work."

"Okay, sorreee!" called Petra's voice from behind the locked door. Molly paused for a second to listen for the plug to be pulled in the bath. Nothing.

She took a deep breath and busied herself around the kitchen: moving Toby's creatures back into the garden and disinfecting the worktop where they'd been; replacing the stocking lid on Toby's stick insect jar; emptying, cleaning and refilling Toby's kitten's litter tray; feeding Toby's rabbits...

"All yours," came Petra's voice through the open kitchen door. Molly had been so engrossed in *Toby's* chores she hadn't heard the bath water gushing down the waste pipe outside. "What time's Dad coming?" she asked, running down the stairs.

"In about five minutes," replied Molly, checking the hall clock while she ran up the stairs. The doorbell rang just as she opened the bathroom door and was greeted by her daughter's mess.

"Come on Toby," called Petra as she met their father on the doorstep. "Dad's waiting."

"'Bye Mom," called Toby, tearing out of his room and down the stairs, two at a time.

"'Bye Mom," shouted Petra, just before the door slammed behind them.

"Er... 'bye kids... " said Molly weakly.

She took a deep breath and busied herself around the bathroom: washing Petra's tidemark from around the bath; fishing Petra's long, dark hairs out of the plug hole; collecting Petra's soaking wet towels from the floor, the toilet, the sink, the bath (why she needed four, Molly didn't know); replacing the lids on bottles of Petra's cosmetics and wiping up the spillages. Her children lived like pigs, and Molly was going to be late.

She put the plug in and started to run her bath, but the hot water tap coughed and spluttered before dying completely. Molly groaned. Not only had Petra emptied the entire hot water tank, but Molly didn't have the time to wait while it filled up again and reheated.

Molly wasn't usually one for New Year resolutions, but this year things were going to be different.

ON NEW YEAR'S MORNING Toby dashed up to Stig's jar clutching a handful of privet – and wailed.

"What's the matter with you, you big baby?" asked Petra spitefully.

"He's gone! Stig's gone." He darted around the kitchen hunting for his pet. "Miss will kill me."

"Perhaps you should have replaced the lid," suggested Molly gently. She was drinking a cup of tea and reading a magazine.

"I thought you'd do it."

"I'm on strike."

"You're doing what?"

"Mother's revolting," confirmed Petra, chuckling at her own joke. "Did you wash my cardigan, Mom?"

"Which one?"

"The blue mohair one."

"No."

"Why not?"

"Because I'm on strike."

"You only went on strike yesterday. The cardigan's been on the draining board since Boxing Day."

"Did you wear it then?"

"No."

"So why did you want me to wash it?"

Petra sighed. "I tried it on a few times."

"But you didn't *wear* it?"

"No."

"So it isn't dirty."

"But I left it on the draining board."

"Then it will still be there, won't it?" Molly lifted her eyes from her magazine and watched her daughter snatch the cardigan up from the draining board and shrug into it. "If you wanted it washing that badly you should have done it yourself."

"But I couldn't put it in the washing machine. It has to be hand-washed."

"So?"

Petra tutted and turned to make some toast. Something caught Molly's eye and she returned her gaze to the magazine.

"Have you found that insect yet, Toby?" asked Molly.

"No," he wailed. "Oh where *is* he? I'd do anything to find him."

"Anything?" said Molly.

"Anything."

"Would you remember to replace his lid every time you feed him?" Toby nodded. "Would you look after your kitten and the rabbits?"

"Yes."

"And would you take all of your nasty little creatures back into the garden when you've finished with them?"

"Anything."

"Promise?"

"Promise."

"He's on Petra's back –"

Petra screamed and dropped the toast butter side down on the floor. "Get it off me!" she cried, frozen to the spot with terror.

"He won't hurt you," assured Toby, taking his time. He could see his pet was safe so was in no hurry.

"Just get it off me."

"What's it worth?"

"Anything."

"Anything?" said Molly.

"Anything," screamed Petra.

"Will you remember that there's more than you who needs the bathroom first thing in the morning?" Petra nodded, flexing and unflexing her fingers as two tears squeezed from her tightly closed eyes. "And will you clean up after yourself when you've finished?"

"Yes."

"And will you stop bringing your clothes down to be washed when you've not even worn them?"

"Anything."

"Promise?"

"Yes, I promise. Now would you just get that thing off me, please."

Ooh, thought Molly. A 'please' too. She smiled and nodded at Toby who reached up and rescued Stig.

"Oh dear," he said.

"What?" said Petra.

"His leg's fallen off –"

"What?" she screamed.

"It's hanging off your cardigan –"

"Get it off me!" she cried.

"Don't worry, sis. It's a known fact that young stick insects can replace a leg if they lose one," he said matter-of-factly. "He'll soon grow a new one –"

"Ugh," she said, dashing from the room, the bright green leg still dangling from the blue mohair.

ON THE DAY TOBY WENT back to school Stig moved out. Molly was quite sad to see him go. He'd turned out to be a real friend. Petra, on the other hand, was ecstatic, and Toby would still see him every day at school. Of course, the children didn't keep their promises, but it had lasted for a few days at least.

No one could see the tiny, seed-like egg buried deep inside the blue mohair cardigan. If it remained there undisturbed, protected by its hard shell, in a year or two they would have their own little baby Stig – a perfect replica of her mother...

the end

8. One Born Every Minute

(This short story has been published in *My Weekly*, *Twee Tales* and *Twee Tales More*)

Izzy Campbell chuckled at the welcoming sign on the door of the 'Bonnie Prince Charlie' hostelry:

No Campbells Allowed

IT WAS THE SAME AT other places in Glencoe. A bit of tourist gimmickry.

While her parents checked them all in, Izzy had a quick look around the place. There was the tiny reception area, a small dining room and a large bar with Toby jugs on shelves and horse brasses hanging from the exposed beams in the ceilings. It was all very old-fashioned with rustic benches, tartan wallpaper and oil-effect lamps. A huge open fire roared away in the grate, a nice welcome on this cold December day.

Izzy decided she was going to enjoy herself here. Her parents had talked her into coming away with them for Hogmanay this year after she and Jamie had split up. Mum thought it would help take her mind off things, but Izzy didn't like to tell them the split had been her idea. Her parents were quite fond of Jamie. She was only thankful they didn't have the added complication of a divorce to go through.

After unpacking Izzy gazed through her miniature window at the icy cold outside and the dark mysterious mountains in the distance. A lot had happened in this area over the years, which probably added to the pleasure of coming.

They were going to spend their first afternoon at Fort William, but there was just time for a quick drink downstairs in the bar.

"IZZY?" SAID JOCK STEWART, landlord of the inn. "That's an unusual name." He served her a small beer.

"It's short for Isobel," she replied.

"Isobel Campbell?" Jock rubbed his red beard thoughtfully. "We had an *Ishbel* Campbell here once."

"Campbell's a common name. They say there's one born every minute in the lowlands."

"No, Ishbel. She was here about a hundred years ago – before my time of course. She was murdered – "

"Murdered?" Izzy almost choked on her drink.

"Aye. Up at the Big House. Young Robbie MacDonald pushed her from the landing to the marble floor as the clock struck twelve. At the Hogmanay party. They were sweet on each other."

"So why did he kill her?"

"No one knows," he shrugged. "Robbie MacDonald ran off before anyone could question him further. Drowned himself in the new loch."

"But there must have been a reason."

"He was a MacDonald; she was a Campbell. They say that's reason enough."

"But the massacre would have been... about two hundred years before." Jock shrugged again. "You think it was revenge?"

"So they say. But they also say he couldn't live with the guilt, he loved her so much. He'd planned it right down to the last detail."

"Oh, that's so sad."

"He couldn't rest though. Each year, at the Hogmanay party up at the Big House – his idea by the way – as the clock strikes twelve, he can be seen on that same landing. Then he rushes down the stairs and out through the door."

"They still have the party then?" Jock nodded. "So where's the 'Big House'?"

"They call it Achnacon House now – after the village that was burned to the ground during the massacre. Good for tourism, so I understand."

"But that's where we're going tomorrow night."

"You might see him then."

"Oh I do hope so. It all sounds very romantic." Izzy checked her watch and drained her glass. "Mum and Dad will be waiting. See you later."

"'Bye."

As Izzy left the room Donald Cameron, who had been quietly polishing glasses in a corner, chuckled and addressed his boss.

"There's another one you've fooled, Jock. I don't know how you do it."

"I just tell 'em, Don. Callum does the rest."

"Your brother's lad still coming up from Sheffield, then? He's usually here by now isn't he?"

"He's had a few parties to go to at the university. But he'll be here. He hasn't let me down yet."

ACHNACON HOUSE WAS certainly big. The grand stone house was always popular with visitors and the annual Hogmanay party was no exception. The long driveway swept through acres of parkland and ended at a large roundabout where cars could turn.

The double front doors led to a marbled main hall with a roaring fire and an elaborately carved, sweeping staircase that joined a fine landing which, in its turn, overlooked the hall. There were several tall oak-panelled doors, one of which opened into the ballroom, scene of this evening's celebrations.

Folk were already dancing to the reels played by a band, swirling tartans of all colours filled the dance floor. Izzy's mum and dad couldn't resist joining them, leaving Izzy to watch from the sidelines. She didn't mind, couldn't do it anyway. She sank into a large squidgy armchair strategically placed beneath an artist's impression of the 1692 massacre.

"Em... " coughed a young man nervously. "On your own?"

Izzy glanced up to see the tall, dark Scot in full Highland dress gazing down at her. He was about the same age as her, and very, very nice.

"I guess I must be."

"Mind if I join you? I seem to be on my own too right now."

"Sure."

His name was Bob and they warmed to each other instantly. He lived at the Big House with his family. It had been his idea to throw the party every year, and every year it was a success.

He told her about the murder weekends and the game shoots – with cameras. She told him she lived on the borders and that she'd come here with her parents.

She even told him a little about Jamie and what a mistake that had been.

"You have a lovely home," she remarked.

"Do you think so?" Izzy nodded. "Thanks. Would you like to have a look around?"

"Can I really?"

"Course you can. Come on, I'll show you." He stood up and held out his hand, which she gladly took. It seemed to warm at her touch.

Before long he was leading Izzy along endless corridors, past doors marked 'private' and 'toilets', into numerous drawing rooms, boudoirs and offices.

"I didn't realise there were so many offices."

"The staff have to do their work somewhere. The estate doesn't run itself."

Until now the music had drifted softly up to them from the rooms below, but now it was quiet – silent almost.

"Must be nearly twelve," said Bob. "They'll be starting the countdown soon."

"Oh I didn't want to miss it."

"Come on. There's loads of time yet. Let's go and join them."

The couple practically ran along the polished corridor. Down one flight of stairs and the floor became carpeted.

"Ten... nine... " began the chant from downstairs.

"They've started," said Izzy.

"It's okay, we're almost there."

"Seven... six... "

"We're going to miss it."

"No we're not."

"Four... three... "

They were now on the landing over the main hall and Bob sharply caught hold of Izzy's hand.

"We can have our own celebration here."

"One... Happy New Year!"

"Happy New Year, Izzy." He pulled her towards him and pressed his lips onto hers.

"Happy New Year, Bob," she replied after he'd come up for air. He released her for a second and she slumped breathlessly against the balustrade. The clock finished striking twelve and Bob was once more against Izzy, leaning into her, kissing her hungrily.

Suddenly there was a loud crack and the timber balustrade broke in two. Izzy slipped and missed her footing, but Bob managed to catch her, pulling her back just in time. He held her tightly, muttering to himself over and over again.

"Thank God. Oh thank God!"

Gathering her composure, Izzy pulled herself out of his vice-like grip. She peered over the banister to the newel smashed to pieces on the marble floor. If Bob hadn't caught her...

"You saved my life."

"Are you all right?"

"I think so."

"Shall I get you a drink?"

"Yes please." She sat down on the top step and he headed down the stairs towards the ballroom.

Completely oblivious to what had occurred above them, the revellers continued to enjoy themselves. *Auld Lang Syne* became *Scotland the Brave* became *Mairi's Wedding*, and Bob didn't come back.

As the first partygoers began to leave Izzy remembered Jock's ghost story, and still there was no sign of Bob.

Then it dawned on Izzy. Robbie MacDonald hadn't murdered Ishbel Campbell at all. It had been a terrible accident – and a terrible mistake by those left behind. Well, maybe they could both rest in peace now.

"SO," EXCLAIMED DONALD Cameron the next day. "You met the ghost of Young Robbie MacDonald yourself, did you?" Izzy nodded. "And he saved your life too?"

"I think it was his way of clearing his name. I doubt there will be many sightings of him at future parties."

Jock Stewart rubbed his red beard thoughtfully. "So you think Robbie MacDonald was innocent after all?"

"No doubt about it."

"Well I never."

"Anyway," said Izzy pulling on her hat, scarf and mittens. "We're going skiing."

"Well you enjoy yourself," called Jock after her.

Donald Cameron chuckled.

"Well Jock, you've done it again. Still, they do say there's one born every minute. You certainly had her hoodwinked. Give my regards to your Callum. He can have a drink on me. He's done a grand job there."

"That's what concerns me, Don."

"What's that?"

"They had some heavy snow in Sheffield yesterday morning."

"So?"

"Callum didn't make it this time..."

the end

9. The Mystery of Woolley Dam

(This short story has been published in *Twee Tales Twee* and *Twee Tales More*)

When the Dobsons moved into their new home, Colin was delighted to discover an overgrown lake at the end of his lane – an otherwise no-through road.

"It must belong to someone," he told his wife Liz over a cup of tea. "It looks as though it used to be managed, but how long ago is anybody's guess."

"You'll have to Google it," she replied, placing a saucer of biscuits on the arm of his chair – garibaldis, one of his favourites. "Or ask some of your fishing chums." She sat down next to him on the settee, nursing her own cup of tea and biscuits. "But I'd bet it's something to do with that big house up there." She meant the riding centre on the other side of the main road. Local rumours had the buildings down as belonging to a famous gymkhana family who lived nearby. "They seem to own everything else."

This was true, agreed Colin to himself. The family even owned the house he'd been forced to move into so that he could be nearer to work.

After their snack, Colin fired up the computer and navigated to Google. A few clicks later, he swivelled on the chair to face his wife.

"You're right," he said. "That equestrian family do own the lake. But the local authority owns the angling rights."

"You're registered to fish with them, aren't you?" asked Liz.

"I used to be, but I let it lapse. I'll see if it's worth re-joining."

AT THE WEEKEND, COLIN walked up to the lake to see if there were any fish in it. The closer he got to it, though, the more overgrown the lane became. He tripped on some old brambles that pulled at his trouser leg. An old angling club sign had fallen away from the tree it had been nailed to and lay rusting on the ground. Above where the sign had been was a crudely-painted hand-written sign warning 'tresspasses' to 'KEEP OUT'. There were similar hand-made hand-painted semi-literate signs nailed to other trees, fences and gates, all saying things like 'PRIVITE', 'TRESSPASSES WILL BE PROSSICUTIED' and 'NO FISHIN'. And along one particularly scraggy length of hedgerow, Colin could see barbed wire.

"I'm sure that's illegal on a public right of way," he mused out loud.

After he'd been walking for a few minutes, sometimes stumbling in potholes or over stones, he noticed a small clearing up ahead. He was sure there was a car parked there too. As he neared the vehicle he could see that it wasn't a clearing at all but, in fact, what used to be a small car park, big enough for about a dozen cars. But it was as overgrown as the path that wound its way around the lake. He could, however, see a fellow camped out on the opposite bank. He looked as though he were fishing.

That must be the owner of the car, he thought, picking his way along what was left of the path. As he went, he fell down more than one hole allowed to deteriorate and grow bigger. He narrowly avoided falling into the murky stream that fed the lake as he crossed both of the dilapidated footbridges. And he kept his short-sleeved arms high above his head to avoid being stung by the Triffid-like nettles that lined the path and strangled the wild garlic.

"How're you doing?" he asked the lone angler when he finally reached his bivouac.

"Not so bad," replied the man, not taking his eyes off the end of his pole.

"Many in?" asked Colin.

Without moving a muscle, the man replied again. "A few perch, the odd roach and some small skimmers. I've caught about twenty or so today, but it's not as good as it used to be."

"I thought there might be some carp in at least," said Colin. "It looks like a good carp lake."

"Aye, there's a few left. Some fancy ones that stay at the other end. But you can't get up there now. The path is so overgrown and they've been fly-tipping. You can't get through – "

Colin waited patiently and with admiration while the man landed a fish. Only a tiddler, but a fish all the same. And when he released it and resumed his position watching the end of his tip, Colin continued.

"I'm surprised the local authority bother paying for this if there are no decent fish."

"Is that who runs it?" asked the man, totally oblivious to the fact that he'd just as good as admitted he was fishing without a permit.

'NO DAY TICKETS' screamed the signs. 'PRIVITE MEMBERS ONLY'.

Oh dear.

Not that it mattered much to Colin. He wasn't the bailiff and he wasn't even a member yet of the angling club, let alone on the committee. Nevertheless, he did feel his hackles rise anyway, and he made a mental note to see how many others might fish here over the coming weeks without a valid permit. It was, after all, completely off-circuit and not on any beaten track. Colin certainly couldn't remember seeing any competitions advertised here, or any results in the local newspapers.

Woolley Dam, that's what it was called. And Colin couldn't recall hearing the name before. No wonder it was a lake he hadn't even known was here.

Colin quietly observed the statue-like angler for a few minutes more, then bid him 'tight lines' before attempting to get through to the other side of the lake. He had a fancy to see if he could find some of those 'fancy carp', but the 'path' was indeed impassable. The area smelt of stagnant water, rotting vegetation and rank fish, so he gave up and turned back towards home.

FOR THE NEXT FEW DAYS, as he dallied over sending off for his new angling book, he pumped the locals for more information – in the pub, at the petrol station, in the post office, on the farm…

"Too much fly-tipping," said one.

"Too many pikies," said another.

"Place has been abandoned for years," said a third. "I'd forgotten it was still there."

"They're putting poison down. Don't take your dog for a walk there."

"Used to be a lovely little spot," said an elderly man. "Little shop there used to sell snacks and sandwiches. It's where I courted our lass. We used to be able to row boats out onto the watter."

Colin couldn't imagine a snack bar up there at all. Did he mean a trailer that sold beef burgers?

"Oh no," said the chap. "Proper plumbed in, like, with foundations and everything. Car park anorl. It was demolished years ago."

"I wouldn't go up there," advised one of the neighbours. "There are no fish in there thanks to after-dark poachers. They've taken all the carp and then they *eat* them," he shuddered. As a coarse fisherman, Colin shuddered too. British people simply didn't *eat* carp.

And finally, when he actually spoke to the local angling club, the news was bleak there too.

"Yes, we've heard that what the mergansers haven't taken the owner's netted and taken out. We're thinking of letting it lapse. You're right, there's no point in paying for fishing rights if there are no fish in there to fish."

"Actually," interrupted Colin, "I doubt very much that it's been netted. It doesn't look as though anything has been that close for years. It's totally overgrown. Who told you that?"

"I think it was the landowner's gamekeeper. Told one of our lads he was wasting his time as his boss had ordered it netting."

"Nah," said Colin. "And some of the local anglers have no problem catching skimmers. They say they've seen carp in there too. Ornamental carp."

"Hmm," said the voice at the end of the phone. "That's interesting. How do you feel about showing one of our bailiffs the place? We'd be keen to get it back into use if there are fish in there."

And so Colin arranged for the bailiff and the landowner to visit the lake and see what could be done.

"I'M MOST FRIGHTFULLY sorry," said the Ponsonby-Smythe fellow from the equestrian property. "We had no idea it was so badly in need of maintenance. We employ a man, don't you know, to keep it all under control and have done for years. It was so frightfully sad, you see. His wife ran away with one of our stable lads – stable girls, actually – and we felt sort of obliged."

"Well," said the bailiff, removing his tweed baseball cap to scratch his thatch. "It looks as though you've been paying him to do nothing."

They'd brought tools with them, but as they hacked their way through the very heavy undergrowth, a scruffy man in a flat cap, dirty jacket, and trousers held up with string approached them, pointing a shotgun right at them.

"Gerrorf my land," he growled.

"Er, I say, old chap," said Ponsonby-Smythe. "I think you'll find this is *my* land."

"Sorry, sir," said the scruff, uncocking his gun, placing it over one arm, and then docking his brow at the squire. "Didn't recognise you there, sir –"

"No. And quite clearly you haven't done a damned thing we've been paying you to do. I'd say your days here are numbered, old chap."

"Ee can't do that," blustered the tramp, priming and aiming his gun at them once more.

Colin felt something stir in his lower gut... he'd never had a shotgun pointed at him before, let alone twice.

"You have two shots and there are three of us, all much younger and fitter than you, man," said the bailiff.

"So just put the gun down, old chap. There's a good fellow," said Ponsonby-Smythe.

Colin, amazed at the total calm the other two men were displaying, was bricking it.

"Come on, man," said the bailiff. "Let us through to inspect the fish at least."

"No fish in there," said the old man. "Watter's too polluted –"

Yet another made-up tale, sighed Colin. Someone didn't want anyone coming anywhere near Woolley Dam, and Colin thought he'd just found out who.

RELUCTANTLY THE OLD man let them through to 'inspect the fish'. Afterwards, the bailiff and the landowner agreed to share the financial burden of restoring and maintaining the lake again, and Colin was asked if he'd like to be the site bailiff, which he agreed to straight away, even forgetting to run it by his wife first in the excitement.

However, Woolley Dam as an active fishery was not to be for some while yet, as it turned out. For on the very first day of restoration, the mini-machinery was moved in and dredging begun. And the first thing to be dragged up from the depths was what turned out to be a woman's body. And she'd clearly been there for a very long time.

The area was cordoned off as a police crime scene, and a manhunt begun. For the former gamekeeper of Mister Ponsonby-Smythe had sloped off and disappeared from the face of the earth. Perhaps his wife hadn't run off with one of the stable lads after all – or even one of the stable girls...

the end

10. Martha's Favourite Doll

(This short story has been published in *Twee Tales Twee* and *Twee Tales More*)

Vicky Masters hurried on her way to work, splashing in puddles whilst battling with her umbrella. March winds had very quickly given way to April showers, and everyone knew it.

She dashed through the shortcut in the square, a flash of something in her peripheral vision, but not really registering anything other than the occasional raindrops sneaking down the back of her neck.

Vicky shivered when she reached the foyer and shook her brolly through the open door towards the outside.

"Halloo!" she called to the cheery receptionist as she breezed past. And when Vicky reached her desk up three flights of stairs, she finally removed her sodden raincoat, hanging it on the hat stand four of them shared in the open plan office. The rain had soaked through to the inside of her coat a little. She added her dripping umbrella to the others already collecting in a redundant waste-paper bin.

"Nasty weather," she muttered to her colleague opposite before ducking behind the half-screen between them.

As Vicky fired up her computer, she gazed out of the rain-streaked window that overlooked the square she'd recently cut through – one of the few oases of green in this part of the town centre.

The ladies chatted amiably as they worked, and Vicky opened up her Facebook – being social media manager, this was one of her perks and she used it to full advantage to catch up on her friends' gossip and news.

She didn't really abuse the facility, she was too busy, but she did take advantage for just a few minutes every now and then.

"Oh!" she said as she stopped scrolling down her newsfeed. Her colleague quickly peeked over the screen but, deciding there was nothing to see here, she bobbed down again, out of sight, and continued her telephone conversation.

As Vicky scrolled down, a shared post on one of the local pages had caught her eye:

Have you seen this doll?

BELOW WAS A PICTURE of a rather old but nevertheless bonny and looked-after doll that reminded her of Hamble from the old television series she used to watch as a child, *Play School*, a little-girl doll with brown curly hair and fixed features. Vicky had never really been into little-girl dolls at the time, preferring the new-fangled baby-dolls that you could feed, whose eyes blinked and who wet themselves.

My daughter's favourite doll has gone missing, continued the post. *And we're distraught. We've had her for years and she goes everywhere with us.*

HMM, MUSED VICKY TO herself. Strange to lose it if they took it everywhere with them. If Vicky still had her precious doll, or if her granddaughter had it, it would be in a safe place and not easily lost. Still, she thought. Each to their own.

The post went on for a little more, but it was the final sentence that finally hooked Vicky:

*** Last seen in or around the Tesco Express, opposite Jubilee Square. ***

VICKY GLANCED AGAIN through the dirty window. Jubilee Square opposite the Tesco Express was *her* square, the one she'd taken a shortcut through only a few minutes earlier.

Forcing herself to concentrate, Vicky closed her eyes and focused. *Something* tugged at her memory.

She jumped up from her desk, grabbed the still-damp raincoat, and quickly headed back to the square. At least it had stopped raining now.

Sure enough, as she reached the wooden bench – soaking wet now, so not a soul was sitting on it – she saw the litter bin beside it. And poking out of the top was the doll's head – the flash of *something* she'd seen from the corner of her eye.

"How odd," she murmured, lifting it out of the bin gingerly for fear of it being very dirty by now. The old doll was wrapped in a crocheted doll's blanket, which at least had protected most of the doll from the other rubbish in the bin, *and* much of the rain. She was still in a sorry state, though. Vicky carefully peeled the dirty, sodden blanket away from the doll and dropped it back into the bin.

She had a long, hard look at the doll, deciding that yes, this was indeed the one advertised as lost on Facebook. She was wearing a hand-knitted outfit in a very old-fashioned shade of mustard. Vicky remembered her own mother knitting in a very similar colour.

Smiling at the strange looks she received from passers-by, Vicky returned to her office and perched the doll on the windowsill close enough to the ancient blow-air wall heater to dry her off without melting her. Then she contacted the lady who had lost the doll.

JOANNE PETERS WAS DELIGHTED to hear from Vicky. The two women met at a coffee shop where Vicky handed over the doll.

"Oh, thank you so much," gushed Joanne. "I thought it might be a longshot posting it on Facebook, but I was desperate to find her." The doll clearly meant a lot to the family. "I've been beside myself, worried sick. She's been with me – us – for such a long time, and Martha, that's my daughter, really does take her everywhere.

"Tell me, where did you find her?"

Joanne paid for the drinks while Vicky related her tale.

"And, to be honest," confessed Vicky, "I don't know why I didn't notice her before, although I have to admit she looked quite creepy peeping out through the top of that bin."

"I expect you were just in a hurry to get into work and out of the rain," said Joanne. "I thought Martha may have lost her around that area. I remembered seeing her playing with the doll, or carrying her. And when I asked her, she agreed she remembered having it then too."

They parted company – Joanne hugging the beloved doll – and agreed to make friends on Facebook and keep in touch.

Back at the office, Vicky was very pleased with her good deed for the day, but couldn't see her and Joanne really keeping in touch for long. If at all...

WHEN SHE WENT TO COLLECT her daughter Martha from the junior school, Joanne could hardly contain her excitement. She left her windscreen wipers with the fan on to demist the glass. The doll was sat on the back seat where Martha would see her when she clambered in next to her little brother on the car booster-seat, who smirked at her when he saw his sister's face drop.

"Oh," said Martha, flatly. "You found it then."

"Yes! Isn't it fantastic? I put an ad on Facebook this morning and by lunchtime a complete stranger had been in touch."

Timmy was still grinning at his sister, who poked her tongue out at him.

Joanne then proceeded to rattle off the story to her daughter, who didn't manage to get a word in until they reached home.

And then she plucked up her courage and dropped her bombshell.

"Mum, you do know I don't actually like the doll, don't you?"

There were a few beats of silence as Joanne unstrapped Timmy.

"Mum?"

"That's rubbish, darling. Of course you like her. She's your favourite doll."

"She's my *only* doll. All of my friends have Barbie dolls now."

"But only last week you were playing quite happily with this one –"

Martha rolled her eyes as she jumped down from the back seat of the car. "Mum, last week was *ages* ago. I'll be eight *next* week, and that's *ages* away as well."

"Well, *I* like her," said Joanne, as stubborn as her daughter.

"Then *you* have her," said Martha sweetly. "She's yours anyway."

And a smiling Martha followed a sulky Joanne and a jubilant Timmy into the house for tea.

A WEEK LATER, VICKY Masters happened to bump into Joanne and her family on their weekend visit to the big supermarket on the outskirts of town.

"Hi there," she said. "How're you?"

The two women exchanged pleasantries, and Joanne introduced her to the children. But Vicky couldn't help but notice that there was someone missing. "I thought the doll went everywhere with you," she laughed.

Joanne laughed too, and explained how wrong she'd been. "The cheeky monkey even put her in the bin, she hated her so much. But it's fine. *My* beloved doll is in pride of place on a small armchair back home in *my* bedroom now, not Martha's."

When they all arrived at the Barbie doll section, Martha looked up at her mother with a questioning look on her face.

"We're buying you your birthday present," said Joanne. "You said you wanted a Barbie doll. Just like your friends."

"Oh, that was *ages* ago," giggled Martha. "All of my friends have Monster High dolls now –"

"Oh, okay," said her mum. "And which Monster High doll did you have in mind?"

"A Monster High Zomby Gaga," she replied quickly. Too quickly. "*Please.*"

"You've given it plenty of thought, I see!" laughed Vicky. "I think your mum should buy one quickly before you change your mind again."

And so, Monster High Zomby Gaga accompanied the family everywhere they went from that moment forward... for a while... And sometimes Vicky Masters joined them too.

the end

About the author

Diane Wordsworth was born and bred in Solihull in the West Midlands when it was still Warwickshire. She started to write for magazines in 1985 and became a full-time freelance photojournalist in 1996. In 1998 she became sub-editor for several education trade magazines and started to edit classroom resources, textbooks and non-fiction books.

In 2004 Diane moved from the Midlands to South Yorkshire where she edited an in-house magazine for an international steel company for six years. She still edits and writes on a freelance basis.

Catch up with Diane today

Website: www.dianewordsworth.com
Facebook page: www.facebook.com/DMWordsworth/
Twitter: https://twitter.com/DMWordsworth
LinkedIn: www.linkedin.com/in/dianewordsworth

Also by Diane Wordsworth

Marcie Craig mysteries
Night Crawler: a Marcie Craig Mystery

Toni & Bart time-travel tales
Mardi Gras: a Toni & Bart time-travel tale

Wordsworth Collections
Twee Tales
Twee Tales Too
Twee Tales Twee
Twee Tales More
Flash Fiction: five very short stories
Ten Short Stories: Wordsworth Shorts 1 – 10

Wordsworth Shorts
The Spirit of the Wind
The Most Scariest Night of the Year
The Girl on the Bench
Dancing on Ice
Happy Christmas, Santa
Careful What You Wish For

73

New Year's Revolution
One Born Every Minute
The Mystery of Woolley Dam
Martha's Favourite Doll
The Complete Angler
Alexandra's Ragtag Band
Pancake Race

Short Tarot Tales
The Ace of Wands
The Ace of Cups

Writers' guides
Diary of a Scaredy Cat
Project Management for Writers: Gate 1

Other non-fiction
A History of Cadbury
The Life of Richard Cadbury

Magazine
Words Worth Reading

Did you love *Ten Short Stories: Wordsworth Shorts 1 - 10*? Then you should read *Mardi Gras*[1] by Diane Wordsworth!

As usual, brother and sister team Toni & Bart are off into history to solve a mystery. However, this time there's something wrong. This time, they land in the wrong place at the wrong time. This doesn't stop them from enjoying Mardi Gras in New Orleans, but they do have to work out how to get back.

NOTE: This novella was first published in Words Worth Reading. Read more at https://dianewordsworth.com.

---

1. https://books2read.com/u/bzdyaz

2. https://books2read.com/u/bzdyaz

About the Author

Diane Wordsworth was born and bred in Solihull in the West Midlands when it was still Warwickshire. She started to write for magazines in 1985 and became a full-time freelance photojournalist in 1996. In 1998 she became sub-editor for several education trade magazines and started to edit classroom resources, textbooks and non-fiction books.

In 2004 Diane moved from the Midlands to South Yorkshire where she edited an in-house magazine for an international steel company for six years. She still edits and writes on a freelance basis.

Read more at https://dianewordsworth.com.

Lightning Source UK Ltd.
Milton Keynes UK
UKHW020649170322
400211UK00009B/722